Peer Pressure Gauge

To Justine, Turner and Grace
~ with love, Julia

Written by
JULIA COOK

Illustrated by ANITA DUFALLA

BOYS TOWN Press

Boys Town, Nebraska

W9-ASL-330
BUILDING RELATIONSHIPS

Peer Pressure Gauge
Text and Illustrations Copyright © 2013 by Father Flanagan's Boys' Home
ISBN 978-1-934490-48-8

Published by the Boys Town Press
14100 Crawford St.
Boys Town, NE 68010

Press

For a Boys Town Press catalog, call **1-800-282-6657**
or visit our website: **BoysTownPress.org**

Publisher's Cataloging-in-Publication Data

Cook, Julia, 1964-

Peer pressure gauge / written by Julia Cook ; illustrated by Anita DuFalla. -- Boys Town, NE : Boys Town Press, c2013

p. ; cm.
(Building relationships ; 4th)

ISBN: 978-1-934490-48-8

Audience: grades K-6.
Summary: When Norbert is less than eager to try new food, he experiences first-hand what it's like to be on the receiving end of peer pressure. Norbert's imaginative descriptions of how it feels to have your peer pressure gauge continue to rise will draw readers in, while they witness his internal deliberation as he tries to let his inner voice shine.

1. Peer pressure--Juvenile fiction. 2. Self-esteem in children--Juvenile fiction. 3. Interpersonal relations in children--Juvenile fiction. 4. Children--Life skills guides--Juvenile fiction. 5. [Popularity--Fiction. 6. Self-esteem--Fiction. 7. Interpersonal relations--Fiction.] I. DuFalla, Anita. II. Title. III. Series: Building relationships ; no. 4.

PZ7.C76984 P44 2013

E   1308

Printed in the United States
10 9 8 7 6 5 4 3 2 1

Boys Town Press is the publishing division of Boys Town, a national organization serving children and families.

My name is **Norbert**,

and I am **namuh** (AKA… human spelled backwards).
I love being me! I like to draw… and I'm pretty good
at it. I love to play handball soccer. I like to hang
out with my friends. **AND** like all other **namuhs**,
everything I eat has jelly beans in it!

Last week at school, my teacher
had a jelly bean pizza delivered to my class.
He passed a small piece out to everyone
and then he said,

"Class, just wait a minute before you start to eat,
I know that most jelly beans are supposed to be sweet.
But I want you **namuhs** to try something new.
So let me explain what it is you must do.

This pizza is special and it's topped with a bean,
That most of you **namuhs** have probably never seen.

This jelly bean tastes just like an anchovy.
I had them put on this pizza so that you can show me,

That you are brave enough to try different tastes.
Now dig in and eat it so the pizza won't go to waste!"

"Anchovies… YUK as in little salty fish?" said Nelda.

Nobody touched their pizza. We all just sat there with our feet in our laps.

"YEP!"

"Well," said my teacher, "I guess I will just have to 'sweeten the pot!' If everyone will just try one teeny, weeny, little,

itty-bitty bite **of anchovy jelly bean pizza,**

I will give all of you an **EXTRA RECESS!**

You can even spit the pizza out if you don't like how it tastes."

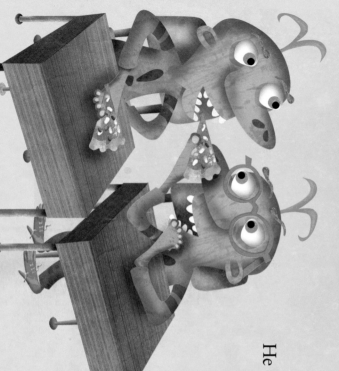

Buster was first to try,
and he took a great big bite.
He chewed it up and swallowed it,
and said, **"It's alright."**

Twins Tommy and Lonny
did the exact same thing.
Then Tommy said to Lonny,
"It's not as bad as it seems."

Nelda wrinkled her
nose and scrunched her eyes and said,
"YUK it's fish!"

Then she took a little nibble
and met our teacher's wish.

One by one all the rest
of the kids took a little taste.

But not me as I sat there with a

YUK look on my face.

"To get the extra recess, you all have to try it," my teacher said.

"Looks like you're the last one, Norbert."

I wouldn't touch my pizza... I just sat there with my feet in my lap!

"Come on, Norbert, try it! It's not that bad. Think about the extra recess and all the fun we'll have!"

"Yeah, Norbert, come on, just take a little bite. If it tastes bad, spit it out... just give it a try."

Suddenly, I felt like I had a **peer pressure** gauge stuck to the top of my head, and it went up to like a HUNDRED!

Peer pressure, peer pressure,
You know how it goes.
It pushes on my knees, and
It pulls on my toes.

It drags me into doing things
That might not be my choice.
*This **peer pressure** inside of me*
Wants to take away my voice!

Then, "NOPE!

I looked up at all of them with my serious eyes and said,

I'm NOT going to try it."

"Well," said my teacher, "I guess I'm just going to have to 'sweeten' the pot again! If everyone will just try one teeny, weeny, little, itty-bitty bite of anchovy jelly bean pizza, I will give all of you an extra recess **AND** a free assignment pass that you can use on any assignment you wish."

"Any assignment?" I asked.

"Any assignment!"

"Even my seven-page social studies research paper on Constantinople?"

"Any assignment!"

"Nope," I said. "I'd rather not."

I just stared at the floor and sat there with my feet in my lap.

Norbert! said Buster...

"Come on, man!
Extra recess **AND** an assignment pass...
Don't you understand?"

"Come on, **Norbert**...
It can't be all that tough."
"Don't be such a baby!
Just think... no research stuff!"

And then, my **peer pressure** gauge went up to like... a THOUSAND!!

Peer pressure, peer pressure,
You know how it goes.
It pushes on my knees, and
It pulls on my toes.

It drags me into doing things
That might not be my choice.
*This **peer pressure** inside of me*
Wants to take away my voice!

Then, I looked up
at all of them with my even **more serious** eyes and said,

"NOPE!

Like I said before, I'd rather not."

"Well," said my teacher, "it's my job to widen your horizons, and I think you should be exposed to all different kinds of food! 'Sweetening' the pot obviously didn't work, so maybe I should sour it a bit!

Toenail Polish Assignment
• 7 pages
• Must include bibliography

EXTRA RECESS

My original offer of an  still stands.

BUT, if **ALL** of you won't try it, **EVERYONE** will have to write a seven-page research paper on the history of toenail polish,

AND

you will miss all of your recesses
for one full week!"

"Come on, **Norbert**, try it! You can even spit it out!"

"DO IT! DO IT!" "DO IT!"

they all began to shout!

"Please, **Norbert**, PLEASE," I heard Nelda say.
"We just can't have our recess taken away!"

16

"And who in their right mind would want to write a seven page research paper on TOENAIL POLISH?"

yelled Tommy!

"YEAH! YUK!" said Lonny!

"It's just a teeny, weeny, little, itty-bitty, bite! How bad can it be? "You can even spit it out! Just set us all free!"

"NOPE!" I said.

17

AND your days of being

"That's it," said Buster,
"I've had it with you!
Can't you see
what you're putting us through?
If you won't do this,
I won't be your friend!

18

'Cool' will come to an END!"

"Yeah," said Stewey, "I feel the same way!
If you won't try the pizza, don't ask me to play!"

"I don't like you anymore," my best friend Freddy said.
"I can't believe you won't say yes.
You're making me SO mad!"

"In fact, **NONE** of us will like you,
if you don't take that bite!
You'll have no friends. You'll be so sad
I bet you'll even

CRY!"

And then, my **peer pressure** gauge went up to like...

a MILLION!!

Peer pressure, peer pressure,
You know how it goes.
It pushes on my knees, and
It pulls on my toes.

It drags me into doing things
That might not be my choice.
*This **peer pressure** inside of me*
Wants to take away my voice!

1,000,000

Two research papers!
NO recess for a whole week!
NO friends!

(I can spit it out if it tastes bad....)

AAAAAAAAAAAHHHHHHHHH!

I grabbed the piece of pizza with my foot and held it up to my face and opened my mouth.

I was just about to take a teeny, weeny, little, itty-bitty, bite

and then....

DON'T BE FRIENDS WITH NORBERT

I set the pizza back down on my napkin.

I looked at all of them with my **most serious** eyes, shook my head, and said,

"NOPE, I'm not going to try it!"

"NORBERT!"

they all screamed at once!

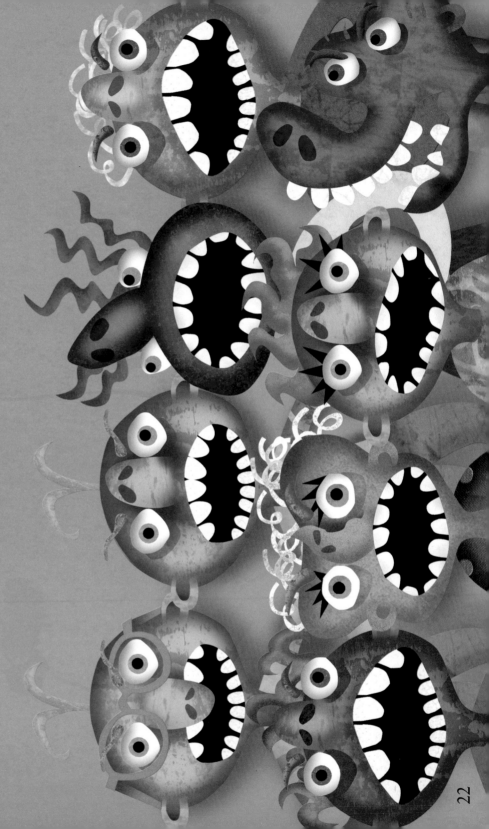

"That's IT!" my teacher said,

"STOP!"

23

"**Nǫrbert**, will you please tell the rest of the class why you have chosen not to try a teeny, tiny, little, itty-bitty bite of anchovy jelly bean pizza?"

"Because yesterday, you told me not to," I said.

"That's right. I wanted all of you **namuhs** to learn what **peer pressure** feels like. So yesterday during spelling, I pulled Norbert into the hall and told him that no matter what happened in class today, he needed to say 'NO' to the pizza."

"Norbert, you did a FANTASTIC job!"

Resisting **negative peer pressure** is very hard to do.
You never can tell what kids might put you through.
You have to be self-confident and show your inner strength.
But those who can do it end up being really great.

Norbert did it perfectly. He looked at all of you.
He used a calm, assertive voice, even though it was hard to do.
He had a good reason inside his head
that kept him from saying yes.
He showed us all how strong he is.
Norbert, you're the **BEST**!"

"How did it make you feel inside when everyone was putting so much pressure on you?"

"Well, actually, I felt like I had a **peer pressure** gauge stuck to the top of my head and it went up to like...

a GAZILLION!!

Peer pressure, peer pressure,
You know how it goes.
It pushes on my knees, and
It pulls on my toes.

It drags me into doing things
That might not be my choice.
*This **peer pressure** inside of me*
Wants to take away my voice!"

DO IT! DO IT! DO IT! DO IT! DO IT!

DO IT! DO IT! DO IT! DO IT!

NO!

DO IT! DO IT! DO IT! DO IT! DO IT!

"Was it hard to keep saying no?"

"it was **REALLY, REALLY, REALLY** hard!"

"How did you do it?"

"I just had to make the **voice inside my head stronger** than the voices from everybody else."

"Norbert, you taught all of us a great lesson today!

Being able to resist **negative peer pressure** will help you feel better about yourself and avoid consequences that might be hard to live with. By having enough confidence to say 'NO,' you can make your life

SO much easier!

AND you can be a great example for others. If you say 'NO' maybe they can be strong enough to do it too!"

"**Norbert**, you passed this very difficult test with an

A+++!

As a reward, I will let you use this grade on any assignment you choose!"

"Any assignment?"

"YEP!"

"Even my seven-page social studies research paper on Constantinople?"

"Any assignment!"

"YES!!!!!!"